TO: DEVON

FROM: KAYLAH

A DOUBLEDAY BOOK

Bantam Doubleday Dell Publishing Group, Inc.

1540 Broadway

New York, New York 10036

First American Edition 1999

Originally published in France as l'Adoption, © Éditions du Seuil, 1999
Doubleday and the portrayal of an anchor with a dolphin are
trademarks of Bantam Doubleday Dell Publishing Group, Inc.

Copyright © 1999 by Thierry Dedieu

Library of Congress Cataloging-in-Publication Data

Dedieu, Thierry.

[l'Adoption. French]   Out for Good :

the adventures of Panda and Koala / Thierry Dedieu.

—1st American ed.

p.   cm.

Summary: Panda and Koala adopt a goldfish from the pet shop, but when
he is unhappy with his life in captivity they decide to set him free.

ISBN 0-385-32634-3

[1. Goldfish—Fiction. 2. Pets—Fiction. 3. Panda—Fiction.
4. Koala—Fiction.]   I. Title.

PZ7.D35865Ad 1999

[E]—dc21   98-17234

CIP

AC

The text of this book is set in 18.5-point Italia Bold.

Manufactured in U.S.A.

April 1999

10 9 8 7 6 5 4 3 2 1

Out for Good

The Adventures
of Panda and Koala

by Thierry Dedieu

DOUBLEDAY

"This is so boring!" said Koala.

"I agree," said Panda.
"We can't spend all our
time just sitting here!"

"Hmmm," said Koala. "I have an idea. Let's adopt a new friend! Follow me."

Koala led Panda to a pet shop.
Lots of animals were waiting to be
adopted.
"It's hard to choose," said Panda.
"I'd like to take them all home."

Panda and Koala finally made a
choice, and off they went with their
new friend.

"He's as quiet as a fish," said
Panda once they got home.
"Maybe he needs a little kiss."

At dinnertime things were no better.

"Our goldfish is jumping like mad," said Koala.

"Do you think he's angry at us?"

"I think he's depressed," said
Panda. "He won't eat a thing."

"Let's take him to the vet,"
suggested Koala. "She'll know what
to do."

Koala wasn't so sure. "I think the cure is to set him free."

And so Panda and Koala set
about preparing their goldfish for
a new life.

"And to live in the ocean, you have to start with a taste of salt," added Panda.

The next stop was the pool.

"There's sure a lot more space to practice the crawl and breaststroke in here," said Koala.

"You have to get used to swimming with a float," said Panda, "even if you already swim like a fish."

Soon the goldfish was ready to
take the big leap. "Go, little fish!
Go find your friends," said Koala.
"Swim and be free."

In no time the two friends had their hands full.

"Talk about a lot of work!" said Koala. "I guess there's no way we'll ever be bored again!"